CATERING KARL

& THE PARTIES OF PURE EVIL

Warren Lane

dizzyemupublishing.com

DIZZY EMU PUBLISHING

1714 N McCadden Place, Hollywood, Los Angeles 90028

dizzyemupublishing.com

Catering Karl & The Parties of Pure Evil
Warren Lane

First published in the United States
in 2022 by Dizzy Emu Publishing

dizzyemupublishing.com

CATERING KARL

& THE PARTIES OF PURE EVIL

Warren Lane

FADE IN:

INT. APARTMENT - DAY

NICK (35), a grungy dude, sits before a COFFEE TABLE. Atop
the table is a OUIJA BOARD and atop that is its motionless
KEY. Nick stares down at the key, phone to his ear.

                    NICK
               (into phone)
          Losing that role made you go
          psycho, Karl.

                                             CUT TO:

INT. KARL'S CRAPPY PARKED HONDA - DAY

KARL (35), in a dress-shirt and tie, sits behind the wheel, a
smoking joint in one hand and his phone in the other.

                    KARL
               (into phone)
          It didn't make me go psycho, Nick,
          I just wanna make those deal-
          breaking Chetflix bastards pay in a
          sinister way and demons know best.
          What's the Ouija spelling now?

INTERCUT PHONE CONVERSATION

                    NICK
          It still hasn't moved since
          spelling out "free." Chetflix is a
          great streaming service though, so,
          you don't wanna do anything too
          sinister to them, everyone uses it.

                    KARL
          Exactly, everyone uses it, I'd be
          rolling in dough right now if they
          hadn't fired me, but they did and
          I'm back in catering hell again.
          Has the Ouija spelled out what or
          who I have to "free" to make
          Chetflix pay in a sinister way?

                    NICK
          Nope, why did they fire you again?

                    KARL
          God, you never listen to me.

                    NICK
          Just tell me again.

                    KARL
          Because I don't have enough
          followers on DingDang, but having a
          certain amount of followers on
          DingDang was never in my contract,
          those greedy number-crunching
          producers just want more money.

                    NICK
          On DingDang you have followers?

                    KARL
          Oh yeah.

                    NICK
          And what was the show you were on
          that they dropped you from again?

                    KARL
               (sighing)
          Nick, you gotta stop smoking more
          weed than you sell, I've only told
          you a hundred times about it now.

Nick sparks up a joint.

                    NICK
          I'm quitting, leave me alone, just
          tell me again about the show.

                    KARL
          It's a partner/cop/action/drama set
          in the seventies. It's called
          "Chimi & The Changa," I played
          Chimi until they fired me after
          only shooting three episodes.

                    NICK
          They stream any of it?

                    KARL
          No, they're recasting my role and
          reshooting my episodes with
          whatever hack DingDang "star" they
          end up recasting as Chimi first.

                    NICK
          Who plays the Changa?

                    KARL
          Scarlett Wynona Portman.

                    NICK
          You hit that?

                    KARL
          No, you know my dick only works for
          people I love and I don't love her.

                    NICK
          The key's moving again.

                    KARL
          What's it spelling?

Nick stares down at the Ouija Board as the KEY moves about
pointing to "S," then "A," then "T," then "A," then "N."

                    NICK
          Satan.

                    KARL
          I gotta "free Satan" to make those
          deal-breaking Chetflix bastards pay
          in a sinister way? I don't get it.

Karl looks at his wrist-watch.

                    KARL
          Oop, I gotta go, catering time.

                    NICK
          Will Maria be there?

                    KARL
          Yes.

                    NICK
          Are you gonna talk to her?

                    KARL
          I don't know, but I really need to
          go, I gotta make that fifty bucks.

                    NICK
          Fifty bucks?

                    KARL
          I'm just fifty bucks shy of having
          our rent, but don't worry I have a
          good feeling they're gonna tip.

                    NICK
          Hollywood Hillers never tip.

                         KARL
               These Hollywood Hillers will.

                         NICK
               How do you know?

Karl stares through his wind-shield at GOLDEN PENTAGRAM GATES
which rest at the foot of the driveway of a HOLLYWOOD HOME.

                         KARL
               Cos they have solid gold gates.

                         NICK
               So?

                         KARL
               Only soulless dicks would spring
               for solid gold gates and not tip.

A HAND grabs the smoking joint out of Karl's fingers. Karl
looks out his driver's side window to the hand and its owner.

EXT. KARL'S CRAPPY PARKED HONDA - SAME

SCOTT (40), red-headed, leans against the crappy Honda,
holding Karl's smoking joint. Scott also wears a dress-shirt
and tie. Karl turns off his phone and puts it away.

                         KARL
               Scott, may I get my joint back?

                         SCOTT
               No smoking before shifts, Karl.
                    (taking a huge drag)
               You remember the rules, right? Or
               do I have to go over them again?

                         KARL
               No, I remember.

                         SCOTT
               You're back in my world, Karl, now
               get up there, we're already behind.

EXT. THE DRIVEWAY OF THE HOLLYWOOD HOME - EVENING

Karl, holding hangered dress-pants and strapped with a
BACKPACK, huffs and puffs as he reaches the top of the
driveway. He spies a WHITE VAN resting before a CLOSED GARAGE
DOOR. Across the van it reads: "Quality California Catering!"

MIKE (40), bald, also wearing a dress-shirt and a tie, leans against the driver's door of the van. He smokes a cigarette.

                    KARL
          Hey, Mike, how the hell are you?

                    MIKE
          Can't complain, Karl.

Karl and Mike fist-bump.

MOMENTS LATER

Mike still leans against the driver's door of the van. The smoking cigarette between his fingers is just a long cylinder of ash now. Karl stands before him.

                    MIKE
          Aren't you on a Chetflix show?

                    KARL
          No, they fired me.

                    MIKE
          Why?

                    KARL
          They said I don't have enough
          DingDang followers. Anyhoo, Scott
          said, we're behind.

                    MIKE
          With me assisting? Don't think so.

                    KARL
          You think we'll get a tip tonight?

Mike turns, looking to the huge hollywood home.

                    MIKE
          I don't know.
               (flicking his cigarette)
          I haven't worked this house before.
               (looking to Karl)
          Carlos has though, I think.

INT. HUGE HOLLYWOOD HOME - THE KITCHEN - NIGHT

CARLOS (40), Latino, in checkered sous-chef clothing and with a BIG KITCHEN KNIFE in his hand, stands at the counter. Karl, still holding his hangered dress-pants, stands before him.

                         CARLOS
          I don't know if they tip, but my
          cousin worked this house before.

                         KARL
          Can you text your cousin and ask?

                         CARLOS
          No.

                         KARL
          Why not?

                         CARLOS
          She's dead, died in a car crash
          coming back from this very house.

Carlos crosses himself with the big kitchen knife.

                         CARLOS
          Dios guarde su alma.

Carlos returns to dicing carrots. Karl looks past Carlos to
MARIA (35), a Latina in white chef clothing and Crocs. She
stands, her arms crossed, as she stares daggers at Karl.

                         KARL
          What did Carlos say, Mare-Bear?

                         MARIA
          He said, "God rest her soul." And
          don't call me that. It's Maria.

Maria pulls out a GOLDEN ZIPPO LIGHTER and uses it to light
her portable burner which stands on the counter.

                         KARL
          Still have the lighter, huh?

Maria looks at the golden lighter--"K+M" is inscribed on it.

                         MARIA
          Do you want it back?

                         KARL
          No, I gave it to you, it's yours.

                         MARIA
             (exploding)
          Why did you run from those muggers
          on our date, Karl?!

                         KARL
          To get us help.

                    MARIA
          You just ran away and left me
          there! You shoulda saved me!

                    KARL
          Sorry, Maria.

                    MARIA
          They didn't rape me, thank God, but
          they did get my fifty bucks! I
          always keep fifty bucks pinned to
          my bra! Why are you here anyways?!
          Isn't Chetflix missing you, Karl?!

                    KARL
          No, they fired me.

                    MARIA
          Why?

                    KARL
          Not enough DingDang followers.

INT. HUGE HOLLYWOOD HOME - THE DINING ROOM - NIGHT

Karl wearing his dress-shirt, tie, and now dress-pants stands
in a line with OTHER SERVERS in the same attire. Before them
stands Scott, he motions to an EMPTY PENTAGRAM COVERED TABLE.

                    SCOTT
          The owner is a Satanist and we
          respect that, right? No Jesus talk
          tonight, I'm looking at you, Tina.
               (looking to Karl)
          Karl, have you talked to the owner
          about alcoholic drinks for tonight?

                    KARL
          No.

                    SCOTT
          Go down to the basement, he's
          waiting on you. Ask him about
          drinks for bar and dinner service
          tonight, be nice and he'll tip.

INT. HUGE HOLLYWOOD HOME - THE BASEMENT - MOMENTS LATER

A creepy stone basement. Karl stands before an OLD MAN with a
long beard who sits in a WHEELCHAIR near a GLASS WINE ROOM.

                    OLD MAN
          Don't I know you?

                    KARL
          Do you work at Chetflix?

                    OLD MAN
          Yes.

                    KARL
          I was just fired from the "Chimi &
          The Changa" series, maybe you saw
          me around the lot.

                    OLD MAN
               (lighting up)
          I produce that show!

                    KARL
               (also lighting up)
          I thought I recognized you!

The Old Man's smile drops then he explodes:

                    OLD MAN
          You were fired?! What happened?!

                    KARL
          Not enough DingDang followers.

                    OLD MAN
          Oh.

                    KARL
          You didn't know I was fired?

                    OLD MAN
          They never tell me anything.

                    KARL
          Why not?

                    OLD MAN
          There's seven other producers and I
          never agree with their methods, I
          was told we're on a "break," now I
          know why. They're probably
          recasting your role as we speak.

                    KARL
          Some hack DingDang "star."

                    OLD MAN
          Numbers is all they care about now.
               (sighing)
          The biz ain't what it used to be.

                    KARL
          How did you get into it?

                    OLD MAN
          I made a deal with the devil.

Karl laughs, but the Old Man just coldly stares back at him.

                    KARL
          Seriously?

                    OLD MAN
          Seriously, I met him at a
          crossroads in nineteen twenty-six.
          I sold my soul to be in the biz.

                    KARL
          Nineteen twenty-six? That'd make
          you well over a hundred years old.

                    OLD MAN
          As a bonus he gave me extra long
          life and a vision of my death too.

                    KARL
          A vision of your death?

                    OLD MAN
          He showed me how I'm gonna die.

                    KARL
          How are you gonna die?

The Old Man looks to his right--TWO BATTLE-AXES hang
crisscrossed on the stone wall. He looks back to Karl.

                    OLD MAN
          I was supposed to be hacked up by
          some psycho in a tie wielding those
          battle-axes, but I prevented that.

                    KARL
          Why're the battle-axes here though?

                    OLD MAN
          Because I scoured the Earth until I
          found them and purchased them.

They were owned by some humble necktie maker, who would obviously and
eventually snap on me and go psycho-
killer, but now the axes are mine.

                    KARL
          And there they hang.

                    OLD MAN
          Yep, safe 'n sound in my home.

                    KARL
          Pretty smart.

                    OLD MAN
          I like you, Karl.

                    KARL
          I like you too, sir.

                    OLD MAN
          Do you know what we're doing
          tonight? What the ritual is for?

                    KARL
          Passover related or something?

The Old Man bursts out laughing.

                    OLD MAN
          That's a good one, Karl!
               (wiping away tears)
          Me and others who have sold their
          souls are gonna conjure the devil.

                    KARL
          How come?

                    OLD MAN
          Have you ever backed out of a deal?

                    KARL
          No.

                    OLD MAN
          Why not?

                    KARL
          All a man has is his word.

                    HOME ASSISTANT (O.S.)
          Sir?

Both Karl and the Old Man look to the Old Man's HOME
ASSISTANT (40) who cowers at the foot of the stairs.

                    HOME ASSISTANT
          Forgive me for interrupting, sir,
          but your first guest has arrived.

Karl looks back to the Old Man.

                    KARL
          So, sir, earlier you said "no top-
          shelf liquor" but you still want a
          full bar, right?

                    OLD MAN
          Yes, Karl.

INT. LIVING ROOM - MOMENTS LATER

In the corner of an empty Living Room, Karl stands behind a
stocked bar. He plays with his ice bucket and scoop as he
stares up at a MOUNTED DEER HEAD on the WALL. Karl shudders.

                    KARL
          This place gives me the creeps.
               (looking down to his ice
                bucket as he hums)
          "Manhattan is with Vermouth and an
          Old-Fashioned is with bitters."

MOMENTS LATER

At his bar, Karl scoops ice into a PENTAGRAM covered cup.
Then hands the iced cup to an OLD MONOCLE-EYED GERMAN MAN.

                    KARL
          That's a good story, Mr. Himmler.

                    HIMMLER
               (a German accent)
          Pleaze, call me, Heinrich.

                    KARL
          Don't forget your scotch, Heinrich.

Karl pours some SCOTCH into Himmler's cup.

                    HIMMLER
          Zo, before Chetflix fired you, did
          you have sex with Scarlett Wynona
          Portman? She's a slut, I hear.

                    KARL
          "Sex positive."

                    HIMMLER
          Pardon?

                    KARL
          You can't call women sluts anymore.
          If they like sex, the PC thing to
          call them is "sex positive" now.

                    HIMMLER
          Politically correct people should
          be put in zee concentration camps.

                    KARL
          Wow, that's messed up, sir.

Himmler shrugs, taking a sip of his scotch.

                    KARL
          'Sides I couldn't have sex with
          Scarlett Wynona Portman even if I
          wanted. I'm in love with another.

                    HIMMLER
          It's just sex.

                    KARL
          My dick only works for love.

                    HIMMLER
          Zat's messed up, zo, who is zis
          "another" you're in love with?

                    KARL
          Maria, she was my girlfriend before
          she got mugged and I ran away.

                    HIMMLER
          Does she know you're still in love
          with her?

                    KARL
          She didn't know I was in love with
          her when we were together, so, no.

                    HIMMLER
          You never told her?

                    KARL
          I was always too scared.

Karl spies the long-bearded Old Man across the room, still
sitting in his wheelchair. He checks his breath before
combing through his beard with a hand. Karl looks to Himmler.

                    KARL
          Hey, you shouldn't be here gabbin'
          with me, you should go mingle, sir.

INT. THE DINING ROOM - LATER

Karl removes a dirty soup bowl before Himmler who sits at the
PENTAGRAM-COVERED TABLE with the OLD MAN and THREE OTHERS.

                    HIMMLER
               (to Karl)
          My-my! Bar oont server, Karl?! Oont
          you're alone, no less?!

                    KARL
          The other server's are finishing up
          your entrees out in the garage.

                    HIMMLER
          Karl: zee catering voonder veapon!

                    OLD MAN
          He's the ultimate caterer, right?!
               (to Karl)
          We'll take the sacrificial goat
          now, please, Karl.

                    KARL
          Right away, sir.

Karl, SEVERAL dirty soup bowls in hand, ENTERS

THE KITCHEN - SAME

On the floor is a pen containing a GOAT and some hay. Inside
the pen, Maria puts a rope around the goat's neck as it
struggles. Karl places the dirty soup bowls onto the counter.

                    KARL
          They're ready for the goat, Maria.

INT. THE DINING ROOM - MOMENTS LATER

Maria and the leashed goat stand, staring at the PENTAGRAM-
COVERED TABLE. The guests and the Old Man still sit at the
table, each at one point of the PENTAGRAM. They eerily stare.

                         OLD MAN
                Put the goat onto the table.

Maria leads the goat up and onto the table. It stands.

                         MARIA
                Enjoy your sacrifice, sir.

                         OLD MAN
                Thank you, Chef Maria.

Maria turns, EXITING into the kitchen. The Old Man grins as
he begins chanting in Latin, the goat's eyes turn WHITE. Karl
ENTERS from THE KITCHEN and casually goes into

THE LIVING ROOM - SAME

Karl gets behind his bar and begins boxing up glassware.

                         MOUNTED DEER HEAD (O.S.)
                Hey, Karl.

Karl looks around.

                         MOUNTED DEER HEAD (O.S.)
                Up here, dude.

Karl looks up to the Mounted Deer Head. It has WHITE EYES.

                         MOUNTED DEER HEAD
                You gotta save my boss.

                         KARL
                What?

                         MOUNTED DEER HEAD
                I'm Tim The Oracle.

                         KARL
                Tim The Oracle?

                         MOUNTED DEER HEAD
                I'm a demon who works for Satan. My
                job is to foresee all things
                involving my boss's future and
                advise him to avoid any
                unpleasantness. I spoke to you
                earlier through a Ouija Board.

                         KARL
                That was you?

                    MOUNTED DEER HEAD
          That was me, you'll get your
          Chetflix revenge if you free him.

                    KARL
          Will it be sinister?

                    MOUNTED DEER HEAD
          The sinisterest, now free Satan.

                    KARL
          What do I free him from exactly?

                    MOUNTED DEER HEAD
          He's trapped in a goat who's
          trapped inside a pentagram.

                    KARL
          I gotta free him right now?

                    MOUNTED DEER HEAD
          Yes, it's gotta be right now.

                    KARL
          Kinda last minute, Tim The Oracle.

                    MOUNTED DEER HEAD
          Huh?

                    KARL
          I'm breaking down my bar right now,
          I have to do a good job, get a tip.

Karl goes back to boxing up glassware.

                    MOUNTED DEER HEAD
               (exploding))
          That's not important right now!

                    KARL
          But I need the tip to make rent.

                    MOUNTED DEER HEAD
          Still not important right now!

                    KARL
          Does this "free Satan" job pay?

                    MOUNTED DEER HEAD
          No, but it ensures continued life
          on this planet.

                    KARL
          Continued life on this planet?

                    MOUNTED DEER HEAD
          Just do it, I'm Tim The Oracle!

                    KARL
          Why're you coming to me just now
          then, huh? Procrastinate much?

                    MOUNTED DEER HEAD
          What?

                    KARL
          If you have the power to foresee
          everything, how come your coming to
          me at the eleventh hour instead of
          giving me a heads-up weeks ago?

                    MOUNTED DEER HEAD
          Okay, I admit I procrastinated.

                    KARL
          That's what I thought, you should
          never procrastinate on the job.

Karl goes back to boxing up glassware.

                    MOUNTED DEER HEAD
          Please, just free him, if you
          don't, I'll be cast into the lake
          of fire by Hell Incorporated, dude.

                    KARL
          What?

                    MOUNTED DEER HEAD
          That's the entity I work for,
          they'll cast me into the lake of
          fire if I have one more screw-up.
          Do you know how many training
          sessions they've invested into my
          boss? Eons of it. They're gonna be
          so pissed if he dies on my watch.

                    KARL
          I work for a corporation too.

                    MOUNTED DEER HEAD
          But you just cater, I oracle.

                    KARL
          Job's a job, Tim.

                    MOUNTED DEER HEAD
          I work for Satan, I'm important.

                    KARL
You won't work for Satan much
longer if you keep procrastinating.

                    MOUNTED DEER HEAD
          (sighing)
I know, Karl, but I only keep
procrastinating cos I hate my job,
the system to foresee Satan's
future is supes bad and slow, like,
I'm set up to fail no matter what.

                    KARL
Just create a faster system.

                    MOUNTED DEER HEAD
What?

                    KARL
Work smarter, not harder, Tim.

                    MOUNTED DEER HEAD
But I get paid the same whether I
work smart or dumb.

Karl stops working, interested in the Mounted Deer Head.

                    KARL
What _do_ you get paid anyhow?

                    MOUNTED DEER HEAD
Six quarts of babies' blood per
week, I used to make seven, but
it's dropped down to six now.

                    KARL
How come?

                    MOUNTED DEER HEAD
Pay-cuts, everyone got 'em.

                    KARL
Workin' for the Man sucks, Tim.

                    MOUNTED DEER HEAD
It sure does, Karl.

                    KARL
I recently got a pay-cut too, but
you keep workin', push through it.

                    MOUNTED DEER HEAD
Why?

                    KARL
You'll sleep when you're dead.

                MOUNTED DEER HEAD
I am dead, what else ya got?

                    KARL
Hell Incorporated will crumble.

                MOUNTED DEER HEAD
Whataya mean?

                    KARL
According to the Bible, isn't God
destined to smite Hell someday?

                MOUNTED DEER HEAD
Yes, I've even foreseen it.

                    KARL
Well, no more Hell Incorporated via
God's smiting means no more job.
You'll be doing somethin' else by
then, possessin' kids or somethin'.

                MOUNTED DEER HEAD
        (brightening)
Oh, do you really think I could be
a big-time possession demon, Karl?!

                    KARL
You can do anything if you apply
yourself, sky's the limit, Tim.

                MOUNTED DEER HEAD
I feel better, thanks, Karl.

                    KARL
Anytime.

                MOUNTED DEER HEAD
But after you free Satan, you won't
tell him I procrastinated, right?

                    KARL
My lips are sealed and I never
agreed to free Satan, Tim.

                MOUNTED DEER HEAD
But all you gotta do is scuff the
pentagram, break its power, then
Satan can get out, he'll be free.

                    KARL
          What's the big deal?

                    MOUNTED DEER HEAD
          The Old Man means to kill him.

                                        CUT TO:

THE DINING ROOM - SAME

Atop the table, the goat still stands, eyes still white.

                    MOUNTED DEER HEAD (V.O.)
          My boss has already been enchanted
          into a goat via a Latin ritual.

The goat looks down. It stands inside the PENTAGRAM'S circle.

                    MOUNTED DEER HEAD (V.O.)
          And he's stuck in a pentagram.

                                        BACK TO:

THE LIVING ROOM - SAME

Karl still stands behind his bar, staring up at the white-
eyed Mounted Deer Head.

                    KARL
          And that's why I gotta scuff it?

                    MOUNTED DEER HEAD
          Yep, it'll break the pentagram's
          evil-trapping power, free my boss.

                    KARL
          Why is the Old Man doing this?

                    MOUNTED DEER HEAD
          Each person at this catered event
          made a crossroads deal with Satan
          long ago. Now, each one wants to
          back out of their crossroads deal
          and to do so they're gonna kill
          Satan, keep their souls.

                    KARL
          Back out of their deals?

                    MOUNTED DEER HEAD
          Yep, they're deal-breakers.

                    KARL
Will Satan tip?

                    MOUNTED DEER HEAD
Tip?

                    KARL
If I free him will he tip me, say
fifty bucks, afterwards?

                    MOUNTED DEER HEAD
Probably, he's a classy dude, but
if he dies no more tips for anyone.

                    KARL
Whataya mean?

                    MOUNTED DEER HEAD
Satan's death will sorta kinda...

                    KARL
His death will "sorta kinda" what?

                    MOUNTED DEER HEAD
Jump-start the Apocalypse.

                    KARL
         (exploding)
This is why you don't procrastinate
on the job, Tim!

                    MOUNTED DEER HEAD
I knew you'd be mad, Karl.

                    KARL
You gotta create a faster system
for sifting through the foreseen
material of Satan's future! If you
had, you coulda given me a heads-up
weeks ago! I'd be better prepared!

                    MOUNTED DEER HEAD
Okay, I'll create a faster system
for sifting through the foreseen
material _if_ you promise not to tell
Satan I procrastinated this time.

                    KARL
Sure, I promise, now what do you
mean Satan's death will jump-start
the Apocalypse?

                    MOUNTED DEER HEAD
It's not the fun kind, dude.

                    KARL
          But what exactly will happen?

                    MOUNTED DEER HEAD
          If the Old Man kills Satan, the Old
          Man will not only get out of his
          deal, but take Satan's place atop
          his dark throne. Then the Old Man
          and his evil douchemongery friends
          will jump-start the Apocalypse here
          on Earth, not the fun kind, dude.

                                        CUT TO:

THE DINING ROOM - SAME

Atop the table, the white-eyed goat, still standing inside
the Pentagram, stares at the Old Man who raises a KNIFE.

                    MOUNTED DEER HEAD (V.O.)
          He's about to kill Satan, Karl.

                                        BACK TO:

THE LIVING ROOM - SAME

Karl, still stares up at the white-eyed Mounted Deer Head.

                    MOUNTED DEER HEAD
          Scuff the pentagram, free my boss!

Karl rushes out from behind the bar and into

THE DINING ROOM - SAME

Karl runs and jumps over the wheelchair-bound Old Man who
still has his KNIFE raised. Karl lands on the table, scuffing
the round PENTAGRAM design. Karl grabs the white-eyed goat.

                    WHITE-EYED GOAT
               (bleatish)
          I'm free!

                    OLD MAN
          Quick somebody fix the pentagram!

                    WHITE-EYED GOAT
          Let's get outta here, Karl!

The goat uses its horns to get Karl onto its back then the
goat, Karl atop its back, runs off the table and into

THE LIVING ROOM - SAME

Karl, riding atop the goat, passes his bar as they head into

THE BASEMENT - SAME

The goat, Karl still on its back, gallops down the stairs and
CRASHES through the GLASS

WINE ROOM - SAME

As the goat crashes through the glass wall, Karl falls off
its back. Karl quickly sits up, shaking glass from his head.

                    WHITE-EYED GOAT
          Thanks for freeing me, Karl.

                    KARL
          Fifty bucks, please, Satan.

                    WHITE-EYED GOAT
          What?

                    KARL
          Tim said, you'd tip me if I freed
          you cos you're classy like that.

                    WHITE-EYED GOAT
          When I get out of this goat body,
          I'm gonna cast that blabber-mouth
          Tim right into the lake of fire.

                    KARL
          Whoa, don't do that.

                    WHITE-EYED GOAT
          Why not?

                    KARL
          Tim's good at his job, he even gave
          me a heads-up about freeing you.

                    WHITE-EYED GOAT
          A heads-up with plenty of time? Tim
          has a procrastination problem.

                    KARL
          I freed you, didn't I?

                    WHITE-EYED GOAT
          Yes.

                    KARL
          Fifty bucks, please, Satan.

                    WHITE-EYED GOAT
          No.

                    KARL
          Come on, help me pay my rent.

                    WHITE-EYED GOAT
          I'm not just gonna hand over fifty
          bucks cos if I do, every greedy
          Tom, Dick, 'n Harry will come a-
          chantin', I'm a very important
          being, far too busy for all that,
          I'll tell you how to get it though.

                    KARL
          Fifty bucks? Tonight?

                    WHITE-EYED GOAT
          Yes, tonight.

                    KARL
          How?

                    WHITE-EYED GOAT
          Ask Maria, she has fifty bucks
          pinned to her bra.

                    KARL
          She wouldn't give me fifty bucks.

                    WHITE-EYED GOAT
          Yes, she would, Maria loves you.

                    KARL
               (brightening)
          She does?! Truly?!

                    WHITE-EYED GOAT
          Yep, plus I know she'll give it to
          you cos I can see into the future.

                    KARL
          I thought that was Tim's job.

                    WHITE-EYED GOAT
          It is, that's what we pay him for.

                    KARL
Ya mean, you can see into the
future, but you just don't?

                    WHITE-EYED GOAT
I'm too important.

                    KARL
Too lazy, ya mean.

                    WHITE-EYED GOAT
          (sighing)
You're right, I have gotten lazy, I
pay so many demons for so many
things that I could do myself...I
don't even know what's going on
anymore. I've even lost sight of my
battle with God, I deserve death.

                    KARL
But your death will jump-start the
Apocalypse, not the fun kind, dude.

                    WHITE-EYED GOAT
Did Tim tell you that?

                    KARL
Yes.

                    WHITE-EYED GOAT
          (exploding)
Tim only resorts to "apocalypse"
talk when his procrastination has
backed him into a corner! Did he
just now tell you to free me?! He
shoulda been buttering you up for
weeks! Was this last minute?!

                    KARL
Um, no.

                    WHITE-EYED GOAT
Are you lying to me?!

                    KARL
To the *Father* of lies? Never.

                    WHITE-EYED GOAT
You better not be lying cos I'll
cast you into the lake of fire!

                    KARL
Boy, you sure are ungrateful.

                    WHITE-EYED GOAT
What?

          KARL
I just saved your life and you're
already threatening to cast me into
the lake of fire, not cool, Satan.

          WHITE-EYED GOAT
Sorry, job's just got me stressed
is all, now, go kill the Old Man.

          KARL
What?

          WHITE-EYED GOAT
He tried to break our crossroads
deal and you hate deal-breakers.

          KARL
True, but I'm not gonna kill
someone just for being a deal-
breaker plus I can't kill an Old
Man, he's even wheelchair bound.

          WHITE-EYED GOAT
He's faking.

          KARL
I still can't kill him.

          WHITE-EYED GOAT
But you're destined to.

          KARL
Destined to?

          WHITE-EYED GOAT
You're the psycho-killer in a tie.

          KARL
What?

          WHITE-EYED GOAT
The Old Man bought the battle-axes
off of a humble necktie maker, he
wasn't gonna snap, go psycho-
killer. You're the psycho, Karl.

          KARL
I'm not a psycho.

                    WHITE-EYED GOAT
          Karl, you're standing in a glass
          wine room talking to a goat
          allegedly possessed by the devil.
          Nick was right, losing the role of
          Chimi made you snap. Go psycho.

                    KARL
          I snapped?

Karl looks to the TWO hanging BATTLE-AXES on the wall.

                    WHITE-EYED GOAT
          Karl, you catered for five years
          then you thought you got your big
          break with "Chimi & The Changa,"
          but Chetflix broke your contract
          and you went back to catering--it
          broke your head, you snapped.

                    KARL
            (exploding)
          Those Chetflix bastards!

                    WHITE-EYED GOAT
          Don't worry, I'll help you get
          revenge, it's deeply sinister.

                    KARL
          Really?

                    WHITE-EYED GOAT
          The sinisterest, but first you
          gotta go kill the Old Man for me.

                    KARL
          Destined or not, I still can't just
          go kill a helpless Old Man.

                    WHITE-EYED GOAT
          Karl, he wasn't going to tip you.

                    KARL
            (exploding again)
          That soulless golden-gated dick!

Karl grabs the BATTLE-AXES from off of the wall.

THE DINING ROOM - SAME

DEAD BLEEDING SERVERS lie on the floor around the scuffed
PENTAGRAM table. The Old Man, covered in blood, stands,
repeatedly stabbing a surprised, Scott, who also stands.

                    SCOTT
          Problem with your entree, sir?

Scott drops to his knees, blood gushing from several wounds.
Himmler, the only guest remaining at the table, stands up,
looking over and down to the Old Man's empty wheelchair.

                    HIMMLER
          You can walk?

                    OLD MAN
          Yep, I was faking.

A wide-eyed Scott falls onto his back, dead.

                    OLD MAN
          People never see it coming and I
          love the surprised expressions they
          give when I jump up and stab them.

The Old Man stares down at all the wide-eyed dead servers.

                    OLD MAN
          The devil may have gotten away, but
          now the night's not a total loss.

                    HIMMLER
          I like killing too, excuse me.

Himmler rushes into

THE KITCHEN - SAME

Carlos stands, big kitchen knife in hand. Himmler grabs the
knife from Carlos then slashes his throat. Carlos drops as
Maria, standing by the oven, SCREAMS. Himmler looks to her.

                    HIMMLER
          Is zat oven on, my dear?

                    MARIA
          Yes, five hundred degrees.

                    HIMMLER
          Get in.

                    MARIA
          What?

                    HIMMLER
          You vill die zee old-fashioned vay--
          concentration camp style.

Suddenly Himmler's head is cut off. Himmler's body, the neck hole squirting blood, falls to the floor revealing Karl. He stands heaving, he and his battle axes are covered in blood.

                    KARL
          Don't worry, I took care of the Old
          Man already. It was a chore, he
          really was faking, Satan was right.

                    MARIA
          You saved me, Karl.

                    KARL
          I love you, Mare-Bear, and you know
          it's true cos my dick only works
          for you. Can I borrow fifty bucks?

                    MARIA
          What?

                    KARL
          Fifty bucks, can I borrow it?

                    WHITE-EYED GOAT (O.S.)
          Only seven to go!

They look to the white-eyed goat now standing in the doorway.

                    MARIA
          Did that goat just talk?

                    KARL
               (to White-Eyed Goat)
          Whataya mean only seven to go?

                    WHITE-EYED GOAT
          The rest of the deal-breaking
          producers on "Chimi & The Changa."
          They've already broken the Chetflix
          contract with you that made you
          snap and go psycho, now they're
          trying to break their crossroads
          deals with me. One of the producers
          is even having her own "back-out-of-
          your-deal-with-the-devil" catered
          event on Sunday. You still want
          your sinister revenge, right, Karl?

                                        FADE OUT.